I'm a Princess

For Anne — KH
For Helen Buckley — DD

Note

Once a reader can recognize and identify the thirty words used to tell this story, he or she will be able to successfully read the entire book. These thirty words are repeated throughout the story, so that young readers will be able to recognize easily the words and understand their meaning.

The thirty words used in this book are:

a	don't	make	pretty	tie
are	hair	me	princess	to
bed	I	my	see	true
care	I'm	nails	shoe	wear
clothes	is	no	tells	what
do	it	one	the	you

Library of Congress Cataloging-in-Publication Data

Hall, Kirsten.

    I'm a princess / by Kirsten Hall; illustrated by Dee deRosa.

      p. cm. — (My first reader)

    Summary: A girl dresses up like a princess and insists that her family treat her like royalty, but her motivation for becoming a princess comes as a surprise.

    ISBN 0-516-05369-8

    [1. Princesses — Fiction. 2. Costume — Fiction. 3. Halloween — Fiction.] I. deRosa, Dee, ill. II. Title. III. Series.

PZ8.3.H146Iaah 1995

[E] — dc20

95–10111

CIP

AC

I'm a Princess

Written by Kirsten Hall   *Illustrated by* Dee deRosa

Children's Press®
A Division of Grolier Publishing
New York London Hong Kong Sydney
Danbury, Connecticut

I'm a princess.

It is true.

Make my bed!

10

Tie my shoe!

No one tells *me* what to do!

13

14

No one tells me what to wear!

I'm a princess! I don't care!

See my nails?

20

See my hair?

See the pretty clothes I wear?

I'm a princess.

It is true.

I'm a princess.

What are you?

ABOUT THE AUTHOR

Kirsten Hall was born in New York City. While she was still in high school, she published her first book for children, *Bunny, Bunny*. Since then, she has written and published fifteen other children's books. Currently, Hall attends Connecticut College in new London, Connecticut, where she studies art, French, creative writing, and child development. She is not yet sure what her plans for the future will be—except that they will definitely include continuing to write for children.

ABOUT THE ILLUSTRATOR

Dee deRosa has illustrated more than forty books for children. She lives on a farm near Syracuse, New York. There are dogs and cats and horses on her farm and she loves them all. When she's not illustrating books for children, deRosa likes to go horseback riding in the woods.